Kokopelli
Drum in Belly

ILLUSTRATED AND INTERPRETED BY

Gail E. Haley

In the beginning was darkness.
Deep in the darkness,
the Ant People vibrated to the
thrumming, drumming
of Mother Earth's heartbeat.

The Ant People
marked the corners
of the Dark World
with four sacred stones.

In the center of the Dark World,
the Ant People built a house,
but the house felt too small.
They stretched upward,
drawn by invisible music
to build higher and higher.
Still something was missing.
The Ant People said,
"It is too dark here.
We cannot see."

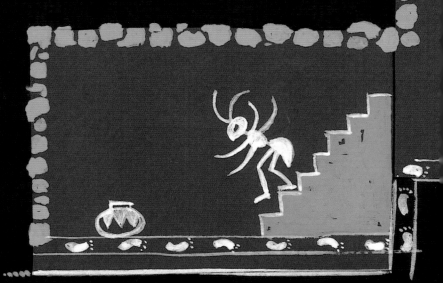

"Follow my flute," sang Kokopelli,
the Cicada who lived with the
Ant People in the Dark World.
The Ant People followed Kokopelli's
music upward into the Red World.

In the light of the Red World,
the Ant People could see the Cicadas
and were afraid, but the drum
in Kokopelli's belly echoed
Mother Earth's heartbeat
and the Ant People were calmed.
The Red World became
their new home and the
Ant People marked the
four corners with their
sacred stones.

Fierce Cat People lived in the Red World. "Thisss isss our ssspace," they hissed. "Do not build your houses here." The Ant People drew back from their sharp teeth and claws. But when Kokopelli played his calming music, hisses turned into purrs and the Cat People helped the Ant People build their houses.

Still the Ant People
were restless, so Kokopelli
led them upward
into the Yellow World.

In the Yellow World,
poisonous snakes slithered
all around. The Ant People
were too afraid to move.
Kokopelli played his flute,
thrummed his belly and
charmed the Great Horned Serpent.
The Great Serpent whispered,
"Take this sacred stone
of peace. It will frighten
away the dangerous snakes."

When the snakes were gone, two shining beings beckoned the Ant People farther into the Yellow World. Ancient and wise, Salt Man and Salt Woman gave the Ant People precious salt crystals. The Ant People ate the salt and became wise, wise enough to know that they needed to reach still higher. Kokopelli already knew the way. His music led them up into the Blue World.

In the Blue World grass grew,
trees swayed, and the fragrance of flowers
floated on the breeze. A river filled
with fish ran through a green meadow.
Distant mountains rose against the
horizon. In the Blue World, Kokopelli
did not play his music. Here he had
other gifts for the Ant People.
From the pack on his back
he took seeds. He showed the
Ant People how to grow corn
and beans and squash.

Kokopelli gave the Ant People
bows and arrows. He taught them
how to hunt animals for food,
but the Ant People fought
and used their weapons to hurt
each other. "Aha," said Kokopelli,
"you are not wise enough to know
how to share. You cannot stay in the
Blue World. You must go to higher still."
"Do not tell us what to do," shouted
the Ant People. "We will decide
for ourselves." But when they
tried to decide, they could not.
They needed greater wisdom.

Kokopelli showed the Ant People how they could dig into the world above. When the hole opened, water poured down. "Now look what you have done," the Ant People cried. "We will drown."

But Kokopelli called
on a wise elder,
Grandmother Spider,
for help. Grandmother
Spider spun a web to
keep the water from
falling on the Ant People.
Soon the hole was dry.

Kokopelli went up
through the hole into the
Green World, playing his
flute and thrumming the
drum in his belly.

When Kokopelli emerged into the sunlight, the Cloud Spirits THUNDERED. "Unworthy insect — do you dare to come into our sacred world uninvited?"
They shot lightning bolts through his body. But Kokopelli never stopped playing his music, echoing the heartbeat of Mother Earth.

The lightning split Kokopelli's old,
dead skin and new wings unfolded
in beautiful colors. The Cloud
People watched amazed.

"Your music is good and strong.
You may stay here."

"I have led my friends,
the Ant People, up through
four worlds in search of
their true home," Kokopelli said.
"May they come too?"

"Your friends, the Ant People,
may come into the Green World
only if they will follow the ways of
the Great Spirit," the Cloud People
answered.

Kokopelli returned to the underworld to ask the Ant People if they would live in the ways of the Great Spirit. They agreed, and Kokopelli played a song of emergence as the Ant People climbed upward toward the inviting sounds and smells of the Green World.

Sunlight touched the faces of the Ant People and shriveled their underground skins. They set foot on the green earth and were no longer Ant People. Now they were the First People. Once again they placed the sacred stones in the four corners of their new home.

From his backpack Kokopelli took many seeds and many babies to give to the First People. Then Kokopelli spread his colorful wings and flew into the sky.

The Cloud People taught the First People dances to celebrate the four seasons of Mother Earth. They taught them respect for all living things and guided them in making sacred sand paintings to heal the body and soul.

The First People never forgot Kokopelli and his music. They made flutes and drums and wherever they went, they carved pictures of Kokopelli, Drum in Belly, playing his sacred music.

Now, each summer,
Kokopelli's children sing their song
by day and by night to remind us
of the time long ago
when we all lived in darkness.

Author's Notes: Kokopelli's Footsteps

On canyon walls outside Mesa Verde, we see Kokopelli, the humpbacked flute player. Across hundreds of years, his music still calls us to dance, and we join him willingly because he speaks to some ancient memory deep within us.

We are amazed that the artist who pecked Kokopelli's image into stone had only stones for tools. It took a long, long time to create the art. But Kokopelli played a special role in the lives of the Anasazi and other peoples of the Southwest. He was the patron of roads and protector of those who traveled. Seeing his likeness on a wall let travelers know that they were not alone.

The handprints that often appear near him are probably the "signatures" of those who left a prayer for safe passage. We wonder whether he can still tell us his story with his magic flute and the drum in his belly.

Kokopelli brought fertility to the people and to the land. Agricultural tribes of the southwest looked to Kokopelli to bring rain as well as babies. In the ancient petroglyphs, the horned serpent is often Kokopelli's companion. The Serpent is a magical creature that has control of the waterways of the earth, both visible and invisible. When Kokopelli calls, the Serpent appears, and rain will surely follow. The frequent appearances of rainbows on walls near the Serpent are tributes to Kokopelli's success. In this story, the Serpent also brings a peace stone to protect the Ant People from poisonous snakes. Salt Man and Salt Woman who give the gift of salt to glaze pottery and preserve food also help the Ant People.

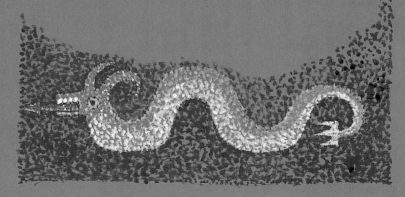

Native American people treasure the wisdom of their elders. Kokopelli calls on Grandmother Spider to weave her web to hold back the waters that threaten to drown the Ant People. It is the Old Ones of the tribe who know how to create the sand paintings that will keep the people healthy in mind and body. The Old Ones carefully replicate the ancient healing symbols in paintings sprinkled on the ground that once completed will be danced away in sacred rituals.

In some petroglyphs, Kokopelli is a hunter shown with the animals that the tribe needs for food. All across the world, ancient drawings have been found with similar images of the hunter and the hunted.

We are told that these pictures are "sympathetic magic" calling the animals to meet the hunter. People who live close to nature revere all living things and give thanks to the spirit of the animals that become their food.

Four sacred stones mark the four corners of the Ant People's world. Kokopelli carries the fifth stone; the stone required to reach higher levels. Four is a sacred number in the art and stories of most Native Americans. It represents four directions, four quarters of the year, the spokes in the Wheel of Life, as well as the four worlds through which the Ant People must travel.

The Ant People represent the journey each of us must make. Darkness represents ignorance. Reaching upward toward the light goes on throughout our lives. Kokopelli's lesson, like that of many other heroes, is that food and shelter are not enough. It is only through higher pursuits of creating art and making sacrifices for others that we learn the wisdom of the Great Spirit.

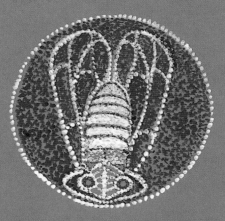

Kokopelli's music saves him from the anger of the Cloud People, but he goes back toward the darkness to save the Ant People. He is their teacher, provider, and protector.

He guides them to wholeness and gives them the gifts that will make life meaningful—rules to live by, seeds to grow food, and little children to love and to teach.

Kokopelli is a cicada—the strange insect that spends from five to seventeen years underground. It emerges from the mud, attaches to a tree, and its old, dead skin splits open releasing a beautiful creature that fills the summer air with its song.

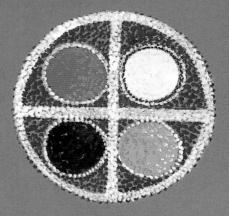

The author wishes to express

her deep admiration

to the Navajo People

for preserving Kokopelli's story;

and her appreciation

to the dancers, storytellers,

and scholars who have shared

their versions of the

emergence myth.

Thanks also to Sheila Moon,

and to the Jungs,

Carl and Emma,

who left literary guideposts

to those who still search

for the light.

To my grandchildren,

Ellen Morgan and Wyett David Considine,

who help me look at the world

with new eyes every day.

LIBRARY OF CONGRESS CATALOGING-IN-PUBLICATION DATA
Haley, Gail E.
    Kokopelli, drum in belly / interpreted and illustrated
by Gail E. Haley.
        p. cm.
Summary: Kokopelli the Cicada leads the Ant People
from the Dark World up to various other worlds and
finally to the Green World, helping teach them along
the way what they will need to know to survive and
thrive there as the First People.
    ISBN 0-86541-068-2 (alk. paper)
    ISBN 0-86541-069-0 (pbk.)
    1. Kokopelli (Pueblo deity) 2. Pueblo mythology.
3. Pueblo Indians—Folklore. 4. Legends—Southwest,
New. [1. Kokopelli (Pueblo deity) 2. Pueblo Indians—
Folklore. 3. Indians of North America—Southwest,
New—Folklore. 4. Folklore—Southwest, New.] I. Title.
    E99.P9H15 2003
    398.2'089'974—dc21

                                              2003005950

PRINTED BY: Codra Enterprises, Korea
Copyright 2003 © Gail E. Haley
ALL RIGHTS RESERVED
DESIGN BY: F + P Graphic Design, Inc.

The art in this book is executed in acrylic paint on colored,
textured paper. Kokopelli and the Ant People were adapted
from the art of Native American artists who depicted them
in stone, pottery, weaving, sand paintings, and masks.